East Haddam Free Public Library
Moodus, Conn. 06469

S0-BYB-625

East Haddam Free Public Library
Moodus, Conn. 06469

NAPOLEON THE DONKEY
WRITTEN BY REGINE SCHINDLER
ILLUSTRATED BY ELEONORE SCHMID

NORTH-SOUTH BOOKS

Whenever she could afford it Maria gave Napoleon an apple. Then, as always, the donkey stood quietly behind the wall. He knew almost everyone who came along the street. Many of them would stroke him and in return Napoleon nuzzled them with his soft, damp nose. He had a good life.

Napoleon belonged to Maria. Maria lived alone with her baby daughter. She wove cloth with brightly colored stripes. Sometimes Napoleon carried Maria and her baby to town so that Maria could sell her cloth in the market. Then she bought food for herself and her baby, hay for Napoleon, and more wool to weave.

Sometimes a large crow came to visit Napoleon and perched on the wall. The people wanted to drive the bird away. "Crows are noisy," they said and, "Crows bring bad luck." But Napoleon never drove the crow away. Instead he always gave the crow a bunch of his hay. "It's for your nest," he said and the crow flew away carrying the hay in her beak.

One day Maria fell ill. She was too ill to weave and so could not earn any money. There wasn't much to eat. Even Napoleon was short of hay, but he still shared it with his friend, the crow.

Finally Maria said to Napoleon, "I will have to sell you, otherwise we will all starve." Napoleon was a strong donkey, and a man soon came to take him away. Maria was paid a lot of money and could buy food for herself and her baby once again.

From now on Napoleon lived in a stable belonging to the man. In the next stall was a beautiful horse. The farmer used the horse for riding, but Napoleon had to carry heavy sacks. In the evenings Napoleon was always very tired and sad. He fell asleep the moment his work was done. Then, one morning, when the horse was still asleep, he was woken up early. It was the crow, gently tugging at his ear.

"Hello," she said. "At last I have found you. Isn't it lucky that I can visit you here?"

Once again Napoleon gave her some of his hay. As always, he said, "That's for your nest." Because he was so sad, he didn't hear the crow reply, "My nest is already finished, but I can still use your gift."

With the hay in her beak the crow flew to Maria's home. She slipped in through the open window and laid the hay on Maria's bed cover. Maria recognized the bird. "Are you going to be my friend now?" she asked. But the crow had already flown away.

Maria felt for the hay. She lifted it, held it up to the light, and saw that it was wonderful golden thread!

Every day the crow collected hay from Napoleon, and every day Maria found golden threads on her bed.

Maria recovered and started weaving again. Her cloth was beautiful. She used the golden threads which the crow brought her. The threads glittered and the cloth looked precious.

On market day Maria had to walk to town to sell her cloth. Without Napoleon it was a long way. She carried her baby on her back and the cloth on her head. That same morning, Napoleon also had to go to town. He carried sacks and boxes on his back. They were really heavy. As he took his load to market for the farmer, he often thought about Maria and her child. They had not been so heavy, and Maria had always talked to him and stroked him.

That morning a crow flew around Napoleon's head.

"What does that noisy bird want?" the farmer asked angrily. But Napoleon knew and was happy. "Maria is well again. She is going to market," called the crow. Napoleon's slow plod became a dance for a few moments because the good news made him so happy. The farmer shook his head.

"Should I give you more to carry next time to make you more sensible?" he asked.

The sacks and boxes were unloaded in town. Napoleon was exhausted. He stood and waited at the edge of the market place. The farmer had disappeared amongst the crowds along with his horse. Where was Napoleon's friend, the crow? Where was Maria?

Maria sold all her precious cloth and earned a lot of money. She looked for the farmer, knowing that he came to market every week.

"I'd like to buy back my donkey," she told him. Luckily the man agreed and Napoleon belonged to her again.

Maria hugged Napoleon and he nuzzled her and her baby with his soft, damp nose. Then he knelt down. This meant: "Climb on, dear Maria. I am so happy to be with you again."

On the way home Napoleon kept looking up at the blue sky wondering where the crow had gone. But all he saw was four dark spots high up in the sky.

The next morning Napoleon looked out of his small stable window. He was happy again. He knew nearly everyone who came along the street.

The crow suddenly fluttered down and sat on the window frame. Napoleon wanted to give her some hay. But the crow did not need any more.

"My children can fly now," she said. "I built a nest with your hay but it was finished a long time ago."

Sitting next to the crow were three small crows. Their feathers were still quite fluffy. They all cheeped and pecked at the apple Napoleon had put on the window-sill.

Maria was weaving cloth again, cloth with colored stripes. She collected wool from the market and bought glittering gold thread from the traders in the town. Her material was beautiful and everyone wanted to buy it.

East Haddam Free Public Library
Moodus, Conn. 06469

Copyright © 1988 Nord-Süd Verlag, Mönchaltorf, Switzerland
First published in Switzerland under the title Der Esel Napoleon
English text copyright © 1988 Alexander F.R. Otth
Copyright English language edition under the imprint
North-South Books © 1988 Rada Matija AG, Faellanden, Switzerland

All rights reserved

First published in the United States, Great Britain, Canada,
Australia and New Zealand in 1988 by North-South Books,
an imprint of Rada Matija AG.

Distributed in the United States by
Henry Holt and Company, Inc., 115 West 18th Street,
New York, NY 10011.
Library of Congress Catalog Card Number: 87-42981.

ISBN 0-8050-0740-7

Distributed in Great Britain by
Blackie and Son Ltd, 7 Leicester Place,
London WC2H 7BP.
British Library Cataloguing in Publication Data

Schindler, Regine
  Napoleon the Donkey.
  I. Title II. Schmid, Eleonore III. Der
  Esel Napoleon. *English*
  833'.914[J]   PZ7

ISBN 0-200-72927-6

Distributed in Australia and New Zealand by
Buttercup Books Pty. Ltd., Melbourne.
ISBN 0 949447 72 2

Printed in Germany

jj   88-200

Schnidler
Napoleon the donkey

DATE DUE		
Je 2 '88	Je 29 '94	
Je 20 '88	Oc 3 '94	
Je 29 '88	Oc 17 '94	
JUL 1988 22	MAY 05 1995	
Ag 11 '88	OC 04 '9	
SEP 1988 21	MR 25 '98	
SEP 1988 28	SE 29 '98	
Ja 21 '89	SEP 2 6 2002	
Fe 13 '91	FE 4 '04	
My 21 '91	JE 01 04	
Ag 9 '91	1 2 SEP 2005	
	OCT 1 4 2015	
De 4 '92	JAN 1 2 2018	
Mr 19 '93		
FE 11 '94		
FE 18 '94		
Je 15 '94		

DEMCO 38-297